for my wise and loving Mother,
and my children, Steve and Cami

Publisher's ISBN: 0-9609888-1-5
Second Edition

Printed in the United States of America

Published by Red Rose Press
P.O. Box 55364
Sherman Oaks, CA 91413-5364

15 14 13 12
96 95 94 93

I would like to acknowledge
all those people in my life
who with gentleness and love,
have shared their Truth,
their Light and their Way with me.

Appearances

clearings through the masks of our existence

by Rusty Berkus

with Illustrations by Christa Wollan

Red Rose Press
Encino, California
1984

from darkness to light,
and back again
to dream, to wake,
then back again
through the ebb and the flow,
we are One in it all.

Rusty Berkus

Wherever you are in this moment,
is exactly where you are supposed to be,
no matter how things may seem to appear.

When you know
you are doing your very best
within the circumstances of your existence,
applaud yourself.

Above all,
forgive yourself

... and,
forgive everyone else.

There is no prescribed Way
for everyone.
There is just your Way for NOW —
until you choose another.

There is no one to compare yourself to,
and no one to compete with.
There never was.
When the Rose and the Lotus
are side by side,
is one more beautiful than the other?

When you awaken
to who and what you are,
everyone automatically awakens
to who and what you are,
without a word spoken.

Sometimes it takes great effort to discover
that life was meant to be effortless.

What we wouldn't give to know
that it is okay
not to feel okay

How would it be to know
that when life doesn't seem to be working,
it is STILL working perfectly?

Did you know
that you could experience
love, pain, joy, anger, death and rebirth
all at the same time and still be perfectly sane?

All earthly pain
is due to our inability
to release what needs to be free.

When you release
what needs to be free,
YOU are freed in the process.

Would you be willing
to get out of your own way,
and let the miracles that are yours
by divine right
come into your life?

Question:
Since you are here to remember who you are,
why have you forgotten?

Answer:
Perhaps you have lived
another's dream, and not your own.

If you know you are not
your sports car, your grades or your children's grades,
your color, your degrees or your spouse's degrees,
your age, your titles or your family's titles,
your body, your possessions or your parents' possessions —
Congratulations. You are Home again.

You stand outside the circle
    and wonder why you feel left out,
unaware that you need your OWN permission
    to join the others —
        not theirs.

And sometimes there are those who love themselves enough to pull you into the circle.

Your loneliness is your Self
wanting to make friends with itself,
Your loneliness is your Heart
wanting to sing to itself,
Your loneliness is your Being
wanting to dance with itself.

Behind all your anger and fear,
beneath all your sadness and loss
is the need for love.
How much love
are you willing to accept from others?

How much
are you willing to give?

Do you love yourself enough
to ask for what you need?

The dignity the world awards you
is in exact proportion
to the dignity you award yourself.

Disease is the soul screaming
through the body,
attempting to get the Truth out
once and for all.

Our immune system is only as strong
as the dosage of self-love, self-acceptance, and self-care
that we administer to ourselves daily.

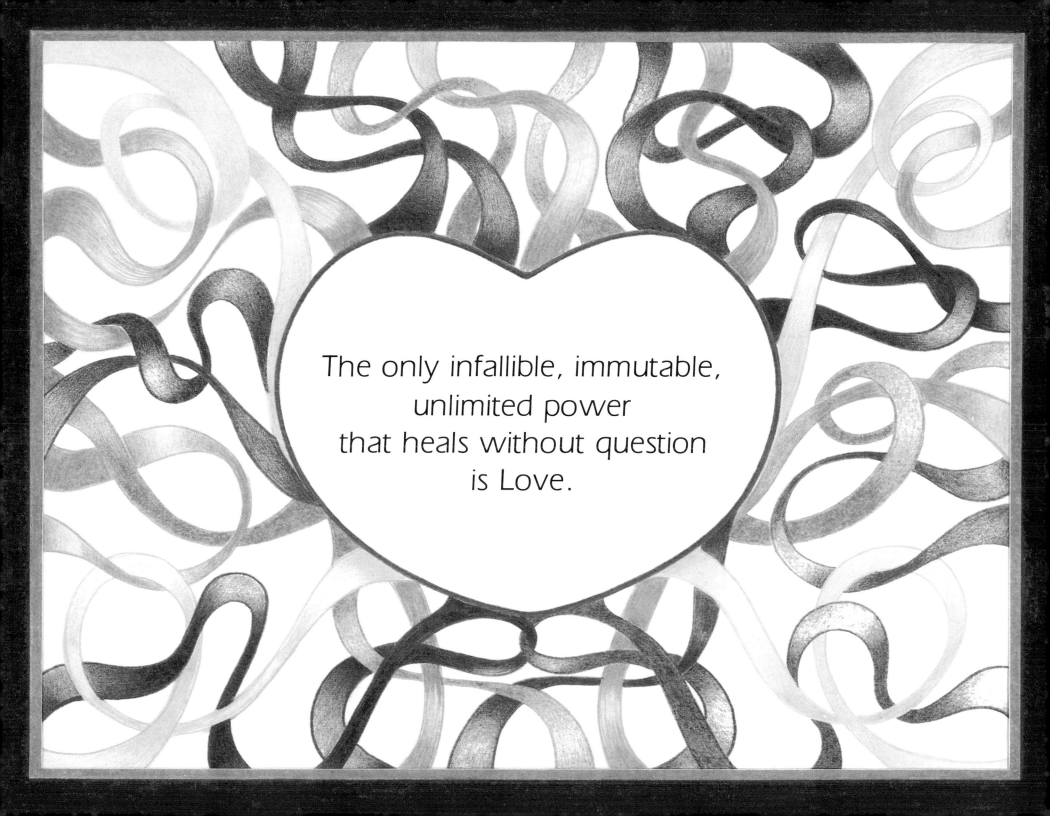

The only infallible, immutable,
unlimited power
that heals without question
is Love.

There is a peaceful place inside
that welcomes you.
A space so safe, so still,
that there is no forward or backward —
only the eternal flow of Now.
Enter this radiance
where the truth of your being resides,
and remember who you are.

Wherever
you are in this moment,
    is exactly
where you are supposed to be,
no matter how things may seem
        to appear.